Tac's
Island

Tac's Island

by Ruth Yaffe Radin

illustrations by Gail Owens

Macmillan Publishing Company
New York

For Greg
and Sam

Macmillan Publishing Company
866 Third Avenue, New York, N.Y. 10022
Collier Macmillan Canada, Inc.

Printed in the United States of America

10 9 8 7 6 5 4 3 2 1

The text of this book is set in 14 pt. Egyptian 505.
The illustrations are rendered in pencil.

Library of Congress Cataloging-in-Publication Data
Radin, Ruth Yaffe.
Tac's island.
Summary: During a summer week on an island off the
Virginia coast, a friendship develops between two boys—
one an island native, the other a visitor.
[1. Friendship—Fiction. 2. Vacations—Fiction.
3. Seashore—Fiction] I. Owens, Gail, ill. II. Title.
PZ7.R1216Tac 1986 [Fic] 85-23119
ISBN 0-02-775780-3

Contents

1
How I Met Tac

IT was the first time we took the bikes to the island and it was the first time we left my sisters at home. It was going to be an excellent vacation. We got the bikes down from the car after supper and I rode kind of slowly, trying to get used to the oyster-shell driveway. I turned onto the road heading toward Main Street and the bay, popping a wheelie. I lifted the front tire, then came down hard, coasted a little and did a bunny hop, lifting both tires up this time.

"I can do that," a boy called from the back of the pickup truck parked in the macadam driveway I had just passed.

I went into a power slide, stirring up sandy dirt, and stood straddling the bar. "Let me see."

He swung himself out of the truck, stood on the back right tire and jumped down. "I'll get my bike." And he went into the garage. It wasn't a summer house, and even from what little he had said I knew he talked Virginia, not Pennsylvania like me.

He walked the bike down the driveway till he stood next to me, a head taller. He smiled, showing a lot more second teeth than I had. "You summer?"

"Yeh. We're here for the week. You?"

"All year." He swung his leg over the bar, rolled into the street, then popped a wheelie, holding the front tire high.

I looked at my watch. "Five seconds," I yelled.

He came over, peeling out so hard that I felt the dust settle on my arms. "Can that watch play music?"

"No, but it's got a calculator and timer on it."

"It's no good."

"Why not?"

"It can't play music."

"It lights up in the dark."

"That's nothing."

I started riding slowly away, not deciding yet if I'd circle around to where I left him or head down the empty street to the bay.

"I'll race you," he called.

I looked back. "Where?" I turned slowly around, coming up even with him.

"Past the cottages to the cemetery."

"Where it starts?"

"To the stone that says Picker."

"I want to see, first." And I pedaled hard past the cottages with him catching up to me. A car coming up the street moved slowly along, almost apologizing for getting in the way.

Picker was a big stone, all right, and it had red and white flowers fastened to an anchor shape propped up in front of it.

"Who was Picker?"

"There are lots of Pickers. Chuck Picker owns one of the clam boats at the dock."

"What's your name?" I asked him.

"Tac."

"Tac?"

"Short for Thomas Andrew Carter."

"I'm Steve. What are you going into?"

"Sixth."

"Me, too."

Tac started riding back to the house. "Let's race now," he yelled back.

When we got to his driveway, we stood even, each with one foot on a pedal. Tac bounced his front tire a couple of times. I felt my tires. They were hard enough, but my knobbies weren't as good as his. Maybe it didn't matter. I tightened my hold on the grips. "Ready, get set . . . ."

Tac yelled, "Go!"

We were even, going about twenty mph on a straightaway. No hills here. I looked at Tac fast. He was staring ahead, serious. I pulled a wheel ahead just as we got to the Picker stone.

"I won!" I yelled, going into a power slide.

"I let you."

"No, you didn't."

"I did."

"That stinks."

Tac smiled. "I'm kidding. You really won. But not by much."

"Not by much," I agreed.

"Where are you staying?"

"I'll show you." And I led the way back toward Tac's house and kept going till we came to the oyster-shell driveway on the right. The house was like a trailer, only wood, with a screened porch, and it was far back from the road.

"What's it like inside?"

"Do you want to see?"

"Okay."

We went onto the porch and then through the sliding door into the living room. My parents were watching TV and looked up.

"This is Tac," I said, looking at the sandy-haired, freckle-faced boy who wasn't quite a stranger anymore.

"Thomas Andrew Carter. Pleased to meet you," he said in Virginia.

"We're pleased to meet you, too, Thomas," my mother answered, sounding awfully Pennsylvania.

"I'll show you where I sleep," I said, and started down the hallway.

Tac followed me into the bedroom. "It's

big. What d'you need it so big for, with all these beds?''

"We don't, but that's the way it comes."

"I've got a big bedroom and a thousand records."

"You do not."

"Want to bet?"

"Maybe you have a lot, but not a thousand."

"Maybe. I'll show you my room. Come on." Tac opened the bedroom sliding door.

"I'd better ask."

It was okay, but I had to be back by ten. Tac rode his bike slowly and I walked next to him. "You talk funny," he said. "Where are you from?"

"Didn't I tell you?"

"If you told me, I wouldn't be asking."

"Pennsylvania."

"Pennsylvania? No wonder. You're far away. How come you're here?"

"We come every year."

"How come I never saw you before?"

"Maybe 'cause I didn't have my bike. We mostly go to the beach."

"The beach? You just go to the beach? That's all summer people see—the beach. I'll show you the whole island."

We turned into Tac's driveway. "I want to see how many records you really have."

"There you go getting picky." Tac put his bike in the garage and I followed him into his house. This was not going to be an ordinary going-to-the-beach week. I could tell.

2
Crabbing for Pizza

I heard a knock and it didn't fit in with the dream. Then a voice—"You in there?"

I opened my eyes and looked toward the sliding door in my bedroom. The curtain hung half off the hooks but it still kept the inside in and the outside out. Vacation places didn't usually come with knocks on doors or telephone rings. I pulled the cover up around my shoulders and tried to get back into the dream.

There was another knock. "It's me. Open up."

This time I got out of bed and pulled back the curtain. It was Tac, all right, somewhere under the army hat. I unlocked the door and let him in. "What time is it?"

"It's late. Hurry up." He took his hat off and spun it on a finger.

I reached for my watch. "It's only seven."

"Only? We've got to go right now."

"Where?" I lay down on the bed and put the pillow over my head.

"Crabbing."

I sat up. "Give me a half hour to eat, first." And I started thinking scrambled eggs with salami and a peanut butter and jelly sandwich on toast.

Tac put on his hat again. "No way. Meet me at my house in fifteen minutes."

"That's too soon."

"Too soon?" And he opened the porch door. "You're only here a week." He went out the porch door without looking back.

There wasn't a toaster in the house, so I had the sandwich plain while my mother made the salami and eggs. By seven-thirty I was done. When I got to Tac's house, he was whipping the net around like a base-ball bat.

"You're late!"

"I like to eat breakfast. It's the best meal."

"Better than pizza?"

"Better than stew."

"Better than hamburgers?"

"Better than—Tac, stop it! I have to be back by ten. We're going to the beach."

"Easy. We're just going down to Hopkins's dock."

"Where's that?"

"Down the street. You take the basket."

I looked into it. There was a tangle of string and shells. "How many lines do we have?"

"Six."

"Wait a minute. We don't have sinkers."

"Yes, we do. Those oyster shells have holes in them for tying the string to. My dad drilled them out last night before he went to meet his clam boat."

"He has a clam boat?"

"Yeh. Next time you eat clam chowder you might get a clam my dad sold to a soup company."

"I don't like clam chowder."

"I don't, either."

We walked past the cemetery. "Can we buy chicken necks this early? I brought money."

"They're no good. They cost too much

and you can't catch crabs with them. Fish heads are better.''

''With eyes?''

''You want me to cut them out?''

''Knock it off. Where do you get fish heads?''

''At McCoy's.''

''Last year we only caught two crabs in an hour.''

''You use chicken necks?''

''Yeh.''

''What'd I tell you? That's what summer people use. Wait'll you see what fish heads catch. I bet we get near a dozen in an hour.''

We crossed Main Street and turned into a driveway leading to Chip McCoy's Fish Market at the end of the dock.

''I've never tried crab. What do they taste like?''

''Who knows? I just catch them. We can sell enough to buy a pizza.''

A man was outside, cutting up fish at a long table under a green awning. The smell was way worse than the pickled herring my dad ate or the anchovies my mother used for spoiling salad. If it hadn't been for the breeze stirring up the air, I would have left, but Tac walked right up to the table.

"Hey, Chip, could we have some heads?"

Chip looked up for the first time. "Goin' crabbing?"

"Yeh,"and Tac pulled me over closer to the table. "They're bluefish."

"You visitin'?" Chip smiled, showing a space next to one of his front teeth.

"For the week." I just wanted to take the heads and go.

"How many you want?"

"Six," Tac answered.

"That'll keep you busy." Chip reached into a basket, taking out two heads at a time, slopping them on the wooden table just as casual as someone counting out apples.

When we got to the dock we tied a head on each line, along with a shell, and looped the free ends around six different posts, swinging the heads into the cloudy bay water. I looked at the flesh hanging

loose and floating slowly with the current. "That's sick."

"That's good." Tac walked from one line to another, pulling gently. "They like the shade."

I swung a line over near a docked row-boat and watched the head sink till the line was in all the way.

"Try pulling it up," Tac said impatiently, and took the string himself.

"Hey!"

"Hey, get the net," he said. "We have one." I took the net and put it near the line just out of the water. "Wait till it's almost out. Then scoop under it."

"I know. I crabbed last year." The string came up, pulling the head and a big ugly crab munching on it.

"Now," Tac whispered with excitement.

The net broke the surface without a splash, and with a quick scoop I lifted the crab and fish head out of the water. "It's got to be six inches," I shouted.

Tac pulled the line and the fish head away and threw them in the water again.

"Just as long as it's five. That's the law. Dump it in the basket."

I turned the net upside down over the basket and shook the crab till it let go and fell bottom-side up. It struggled furiously till it hit the side and tipped over. "We need a cover, or it'll get out."

Tac took his shirt off. "Use this."

We took turns working the lines and net and in one hour we had eleven crabs. "You were right about the fish heads."

"I know."

It was getting hot, and we sat on the edge of the dock, letting the lines hang in the water. By now they were covered with stringy green stuff, and some of the fish heads were tangled in seaweed. I was anxious to go to the beach. "One more and I want to leave."

"We've got to sell them."

"Who'll buy them?"

"What about your parents?"

"They'll make me eat them."

Tac started checking the lines. "They like crab?"

"Yeh."

"We'll trade them crabs for pizza."

"Excellent."

"Get the net. I have one." And he pulled the slimy line up till we saw the crab. When it was in the basket with the others, we untied the lines, rolled them up, and threw the fish heads into the bay.

When we got back to the house, we talked about the trade. "Don't you like crab?" my mother asked Tac.

"No, ma'am, I just like catching them."

Ma'am! That was sure Virginia talk.

"We'd rather have pizza," I said.

"It's a deal." My father laughed. Then he turned to me. "You have to get ready for the beach. Do you want to come, Tac?"

"I'll check." And he started out the door.

"Wait," my mother called. "What should we do with the crabs?"

"Just dump them in the 'frigerator." And he was gone.

My mother looked at me. "Live?"

"I'll do it." Maybe you had to watch the claws, but that was better than handling bluefish heads. I sure was glad I was having pizza for supper.

3
Tac's Island
Inside Out

WE sat on the floor of the screened porch, finishing up the last of the pepperoni pizza. The farther away from crabs I was, the better.

"I'll show you my school," Tac said.

"It's summer."

"So?"

"Where is it?"

"At the end of Inlet Road."

"How far is it to the end?"

"About two miles, an easy ride."

I picked up the paper plates holding the pizza crusts and Tac picked up the soda cans. We walked around back to the barrel.

I knew some things about the island. It was long and skinny like a lot of other islands in the ocean just off the Virginia coast. Waves pounded the ocean side, but the bay water between the islands and the mainland was protected and calm. I knew the sand. I knew when the waves were just right for jumping. I knew about sunburns during the day and sunsets on the bay. Now Tac wanted to show me his school. It was like turning a shirt inside out when you took it off. You saw it a whole different way. And then there was Tac. He was different, too. I still wasn't sure I liked him.

We had about an hour before dark. I followed behind Tac through town, and when we turned onto Inlet Road I came up next to him. A white bird with a long neck stood stock-still in a pool next to the road, watching us. "Is that an egret or a heron?" I asked Tac.

"An egret. Don't you know the difference between an egret and a great blue heron yet? Don't they have them in Pennsylvania?"

"That's dumb. They're shore birds."

"You don't have any shore?"

"Just the Lehigh River moving through town. Philadelphia's got a harbor. That's one and a half hours south of us."

"The Liberty Bell's there, isn't it?"

"Yeh."

"Have you ever seen it?"

"Lots of times."

"What's it look like?"

"A big bell with a crack, and writing on it we had to memorize for school."

"What is it?"

I took my hands off the handlebars and spread them out as if I were blessing the world. In my most solemn voice, I said, " 'Proclaim Liberty throughout all the Land unto all the Inhabitants Thereof.' It's from the Bible."

"Someday I'm going to see the Liberty Bell."

Up ahead, I recognized two of the lifeguards running. "That's Dan," I said, looking at the tall lean body with shoulders that seemed as wide as my arms were long. A shorter figure of a girl ran next to him, a braid bouncing up and down on her back.

"You know him?"

"He's the one I run with on the beach. I go maybe two miles with him. He has to go three every day. That's the rule."

"He's my gym teacher."

"At school?"

We came up even with them and Tac called out, "Hi, Mr. McCormick."

Dan turned and smiled. "Hi, Tac." Then he smiled at me. "Steve, glad to see you back this year. You going to run with me tomorrow morning?" They didn't break their pace.

"What time?"

"About half an hour after I get my station set up. Nine-thirty should be about right. Are you going to run, too, Tac?"

"I don't know. We'll see you at the beach." And Tac did a wheelie and pulled ahead.

The school was around the next bend in the road. It was one-story brick with windows wrapped around the two sides I could see.

"I never thought about a school here,"
I said to Tac.

"How come?"

"Because it's a summer place."

Tac got mad. "No, it's not just a summer place," he yelled. "You better remember we have winter, too, and spring and fall, and after all you vacation people go, it's our island. We have school. We have—"

"Okay, okay. I'm sorry. It's for all year and not just for us when the sun is hot." I rode away from Tac to the far side of the parking lot, doing two bunny hops on the way. This was Tac's island and I'd better remember that. I turned and headed back toward Tac, who was circling slowly near the front entrance. He was as much a part of this island as the waves and sand and maybe even the pesty mosquitoes.

"I don't like you," Tac said.

"I said I'm sorry."

"How do I know?"

"I don't say I'm sorry unless I mean it," I yelled.

"I hear you," Tac yelled back. "Do you want to see where my room was this year?" He got off his bike, letting it drop on its side.

We walked around back. There was a big pond just beyond the cut grass, and tall trees beyond the pond.

"Over here," he called, and we looked into a room that didn't know summer except for the undersides of chairs and newspaper-covered book shelves.

"I used to sit near the window wall and look out over the pond. The snow geese were the prettiest in January. I'd see deer run by, too."

I looked out over the pond again, trying to picture the snow geese flying up from the water. Going to school here in winter maybe wasn't any easier than going to school here in summer would be. How could you think about reading and math in a place like this? "It's nice," I said.

"Sure it is," Tac answered. "It's getting dark. We'd better go."

We got our bikes and pedaled back toward town. That same white bird was standing stock-still in the same pool we saw him in before. "That stupid egret is still standing there," I said.

"You remembered the name."

"Of course I did." And I decided that getting to know Tac's island inside out was going to be fun.

4
The Rescue

THE next morning we rode along the beach road in air that was misty soft. Cars passed us slowly, and a few fishermen turned to look at us but didn't even smile. The mist was thicker in the parking lot and we saw fog brushing the tops of the barrier dunes that were pushed into place by bulldozers to keep the ocean where it belonged. In a storm, waves could break through to the bay, but today they didn't send any drum roll signals from the shoreline. We locked the bikes to the rack not far from a couple of cars. A seagull perched on a fence post watching us, but otherwise we were alone.

"How are you going to run in fog?" Tac said as he pulled his hat down close to his ears.

"There's not much, just on the top of the dunes."

"That's what you think." And he started up the wooden steps that crossed like a bridge over the dunes to the beach. I followed him.

When we got to the top step we stopped suddenly, as if a wall were holding us back. "I don't see the water."

"I told you. It'll take a while for this to burn off. You don't go down into it, either, or you may not get back."

"I've been in fog."

"Like potato soup?"

"Potato soup? Do you eat potato soup?"

"It's good. But you don't go running in it."

I looked toward the lifeguard hut but I couldn't see it. It was near the next set of steps, I knew. We could just about see the sign that posted tides for the week, and I walked down some steps toward it.

Tac stopped me. "Where you going?"

"I want to read the tide sign. High tide's at nine-thirty. It's coming in."

"Almost there, with a good drop-off, deep almost as soon as you walk in."

The sounds were soft in the fog. Birds talked to each other and I called them all gulls, while Tac tried to teach me about terns. "You have to stay clear of them when they have eggs," he warned, "or else they'll go pecking your head to scare you away."

"Where are their eggs?"

"In the dunes in a little hollow."

"Have you ever seen them?"

"Sure. Would have gotten my head made into a salt shaker except for my hat."

"That's why you always wear it?"

"It's from my brother. He sent it from the army. It's too late in summer for terns' eggs."

"Come on, let's go down to the water." I started walking away.

"You don't listen, do you? How are you going to know which way is back?"

"The beach isn't that big."

"Pick out landmarks. That's what you have to do."

"The tide sign is one."

"Okay, I'll stand near the sign. You

walk straight down till you can barely see it and stop.''

I paced off the distance, turning every other step, checking the sign and Tac, who was becoming a dim shadow next to it. When I got as far as I dared go, I said, ''Okay.''

Tac didn't answer.

''Tac, I said okay.''

''Are you scared?'' I heard the shadow call.

''Cut it out. Can you see me?''

''A little.''

''Come on.''

Tac began to look like a real person as he came toward me. ''You don't know the shore. You have to be a little afraid of the fog. In a boat, you'd be.''

Just then we heard sharp voices, too rushed to make sense of. ''That's Mr. McCormick,'' Tac said. ''Something's wrong.'' We ran back to the dunes and along them toward the voices. The lifeguard hut started taking shape before us, and we saw Dan and the other lifeguard with a woman who couldn't keep still.

"What's the matter?" Tac shouted.

"Her little boy wandered away from their camper and she thinks he may be on the beach."

"My husband started looking"—she turned one way, then another—"but I don't know where."

Dan took charge. "More lifeguards should be here in a few minutes. Nobody will be going in the water, so they won't need us. Margie," he said to the other guard, "write a note to Greg and Jeff saying we're going after a lost child. Then call the police from the hut and have them get volunteers to help us. If only the fog would lift."

The woman stood sobbing. "He's afraid, I know."

"You may be more afraid than he is," Dan said, trying to ease her mind.

"How old is he?" I asked.

"Two." And she started crying again.

"I'm glad you're here," Dan said to us. "Will you help?"

"What should we do?" Tac didn't show he was afraid of the fog.

"Stay together and run along the edge of the dune. Don't go toward the water, understand? I don't want you to lose your bearings. Call out Jimmy's name and look around you, one to one side, the other to the other. Steve, do you have your watch on?"

"I was going to time our running."

"Good. What's your average time for an easy mile?"

"About seven minutes."

"Better make it a little slower so Tac can keep pace."

Tac got mad. "I can keep pace."

"Keep calm. You head down the beach and in eight minutes turn back. We'll know you covered a mile. Report back to the hut. It'll be about sixteen to twenty minutes. If you have to slow down, do it. I don't want you in trouble."

Just then, Margie came out of the hut. "I called. There'll be people out in about twenty minutes."

"Okay, boys, get going. Margie and I will go down to the water and head in opposite directions. Mrs. Singer, you come down with us and be our marker. We'll know when we're even with the hut if you stay in one place."

Tac and I started running, Tac faster than me. "Slow down. You won't be able to keep up the pace." I knew that. Long distance was my strength, and you had to take it a little slower. Someday I'd be in the Boston Marathon, even though anybody could beat me at short distances.

We started calling Jimmy's name. First me, then Tac, trying not to break the rhythm of our running as we looked around, forcing the fog back with every step. I checked my watch about every minute.

Tac was edgy and out of breath. "How far have we gone?"

"About a quarter of a mile. Two minutes."

"You like to run?" And he called out Jimmy's name.

"Not like this."

"He could be drowned by now."

"Stop it." And I called out "Jimmy" as loudly as I could, letting the end of his name trail off and get lost in the stillness of the air. ``Why isn't there any wind?''

``That's why the fog's still sitting on the beach.''

I listened. All I heard were the arguing sounds made by the gulls. I looked at my watch again and another minute had gone by. ``Once when I was seven I got lost,'' I remembered, ``on a mountain near home.''

``You have mountains in Pennsylvania?''

``Sure.'' We didn't look at each other, straining to see Jimmy. ``I took the wrong trail, an old one.''

``Who found you?''

``My dad.''

``Did you cry?''

``Not until we got back to the car. Then I did.''

Tac was keeping up. I looked at my watch again. ``We've gone a little more than half a mile.''

Then all of a sudden I saw a shape, bigger than a gull, sitting on the sand. ``Slow down. Look over there.'' We walked toward the figure. ``Jimmy?''

He was sitting on the sand with his

legs bent in close to his body. There were shore birds near him, almost like watchmen.

"Sandpipers, you scat," Tac said.

Jimmy looked startled. Then he smiled. "Birds." He pointed.

"Jimmy," I said, "we'll go find Mommy."

"Find Mommy," he repeated. "Find Mommy," and he took my hand.

When we got back to the hut, the search party was getting ready to start out. The fog was lifting enough to see the lifeguard stands, and Jimmy was fine till he saw his mother. Then he started to cry. She scooped him up and rocked him back and forth.

Dan looked relieved. "Thanks, guys."

Then Jimmy's mother said, "I want to give you boys something for finding Jimmy." And she reached into her pocket, pulling out a ten-dollar bill. "Would you share this?"

"Thank you, ma'am," Tac said in his most polite Virginia voice as he took the money. I said thanks, too, and we ran up the stairs.

"I know where we can get some really good shakes," Tac said, "unless you want to stick around and run with Mr. McCormick."

"No way. I did enough running already. Do they have thirty-two ounce sodas?"

"Don't be picky." And we ran up and over the dune steps to get our bikes.

5
The Treasure

THE next day, Tac went to visit his Gram and Gramps on the mainland, south a little way. We went to the beach and I picked up shells and played in the water, but it wasn't much fun with just my parents. I was worrying that Tac was tired of me and wanted to get away, but after supper I heard a knock on the door and saw him standing there.

"I'll show you a real hill," he said first thing.

"How high?"

"Over my head."

"That's not much. There aren't any real hills down here."

"What do you call real hills?"

"Way higher than a house. Way higher than the top of those trees outside in the yard. So high it takes a day to climb them."

"You have hills like that near your house?"

"Yup."

"Anyway, you're not there, and my hill's good for jumps and a lookout."

"How far is it?"

"It's down the Pine Road."

We talked to my father about our going.

"It's pretty dark there at night," he said. "Tomorrow morning would be a better time."

"It's good now," Tac said.

"Tomorrow," my father repeated, and that was that.

In the morning Tac came by at seven-thirty. He had his binoculars with him. We rode along the Pine Road and turned off onto a trail. "How far did you say it was?"

"We'll get to it. You have to be patient. Don't you know that?"

I slapped my leg, trying to get back at a mosquito. "Why didn't you tell me to put on insect repellent?"

"The bugs aren't bad."

"Are you kidding? We'd better get there soon."

"It's just around the bend."

The pines were all around us, holding onto their green needles and letting the dead brown ones carpet the path. Between the straight trunks, thorny vines twisted and bent with their own way of saying "Keep Out."

"I see it," Tac said, veering off the path to the left.

"That's a hill?"

"Come on." Tac pedaled up the slight grade of the spongy soil and I followed him. "Now look over there." And he pointed through the trees to the clearing you couldn't see from the path.

The water of the cove lapped the narrow beach. "I didn't know we were close to water."

"Everything's close to water. That's my secret beach. There's supposed to be treasure buried here, too."

"From pirates?"

"Of course. They robbed the ships going along the coast and snuck into the cove when nobody was around.''

I looked down at the mound I was standing on that Tac called a hill. ''Maybe it's here.''

''Nobody ever found anything. Let's go down to the beach.''

We left our bikes and slid down the pine needles into the thorns. ''I don't care about a skinny cove beach.''

''Yes, you do. You're just not tough.''

I wiped some blood from the scratch on my leg. ''Are there mosquitoes down there, too?''

''Just horseshoe crabs.''

We pushed aside the last thorny vines and stepped onto the smooth sand, still wet from high tide. The beach curved around the edge of the trees, and where water had eaten away at the soil holding their roots, dead gray trunks lay across the sand like track hurdles. In between them, upside down or right-side up, were horseshoe crabs.

I held my nose. ''The smell is gross.''

Tac nudged one and it started to move. ''This one's alive.'' He picked it up by its spear and tossed it into the water with a loud plop.

"Why didn't the spear come off?"

"They're tough." Tac turned over another shell with his foot and it was empty. "Clean empty Look here. The crab unzipped his outside skeleton and made a new one."

I flipped over another shell nearby. Flies and I don't know what else flew away from it.

Tac looked away in disgust. "Gulls pecked at that one. They just had a dinner of juicy crab and left a mess for the bugs."

"That's not right."

"Yes, it is. Horseshoe crabs eat clams. Now you'll say, 'poor clams.' "

"No, I won't. You don't swim here, do you?"

"You kidding? With all these crabs? I hunt for treasure."

"I thought you said nobody ever found any."

"Not buried treasure, but there's treasure here. I'll show you."

"Where?"

Tac took off his army hat and put it on a branch of a dead pine fallen across the beach where we were standing. "We have to mark where we left the trail."

"Some trail."

"You know what? I don't like you today. Maybe I won't show you the treasure."

"C'mon. Just show me."

Tac vaulted over the tree trunk. We made our way along the beach, our footprints gigantic next to the tracks made by birds' claws and animal paws. Two arms of land cradled the water of the cove, keeping it quiet and apart from the noisy ocean on one side and the busy town on the bay side. Pirates could come here and steal away without anybody knowing, I thought.

Tac put his hand on my arm as we came to the bend in the beach at the edge of the cove. The land had been rising next to us like a ramp, till here there was a twenty-foot bank. "Now you have to be quiet."

"Why?"

"You want to see the treasure, don't you?"

"You'd better tell me more or I'll start shouting."

"Your loss. You just go shout and I'll never take you to any of my secret places again."

"Okay. Okay. Now what?"

"We have to climb up the bank along this fallen trunk and into the trees a little to hide."

"Mosquitoes are there."

"It's worth it. You take the binoculars." And Tac started climbing, finding stubs of the trunk's branches to step on.

I put the binocular strap around my neck and followed him up.

At the top, Tac whispered, "Now look down at the beach around the bend." I started walking a little closer to the edge, and Tac grabbed me. "Stay down."

I gave him a funny look. "This better be good." We were at the edge of the trees right near the bank. A mosquito settled on my cheek and I slapped it.

"I told you to be quiet. Now look down at the beach."

I leaned forward enough to see the sand, which was about thirty feet below

here, facing water away from the cove but not quite free enough for waves. There was treasure down there, all right.

I smiled at Tac and lifted the binoculars to my eyes. "Beautiful!"

Tac grabbed at the strap around my neck. "Let me see."

"How do they get there?"

"In boats. See them out there?"

One of the girls sat up and started smearing suntan oil all over her body. "Wow!"

"I can tell you've never seen a naked girl."

"I opened the door once when one of my sisters was undressed. She started throwing things at me."

"That doesn't count." Tac pointed the binoculars farther down the beach. "Look at that one." He gave me back the binoculars.

We stayed there watching till I had more mosquito bites than teeth in my mouth. When we got back to the summer house, my mother looked at us in horror. "What happened to you two? You're filthy, and eaten alive."

"Tac showed me where some treasure was supposed to be hidden."

"By pirates, I suppose."

"Yes, ma'am."

"Tac, you know stories like that usually aren't true."

"We had a good time looking, anyway," I said, which was true, and I winked at Tac as we walked down the hall to the bathroom to wash up.

6
Turning Pro

THE week was going too fast, and it didn't help that I had to take time out to practice the trumpet. Up till now I hadn't told Tac because I thought he'd laugh, but he showed up just when my mom said I couldn't put it off any longer.

"How come you have to practice every day?" he asked.

"'Cause I have to."

"That's no reason."

"If I don't, I can't ride my bike."

"That's a reason."

I took the trumpet out of the case and slowly put the mouthpiece in. Tac sat on the edge of the bed and watched. I played a C scale up and left it there. Then I played some notes using the first valve.

Nobody else I knew had to practice on vacation. We even took the trumpet when we went camping. I had to walk way out in a pasture once, away from the tents, so I wouldn't bother anyone except the cows. It was smelly, and the stupid cows didn't even want to listen. They just turned and lumbered away, swishing their tails.

"Listen to this." I tightened my lips and blew.

"Yow! That's too high." Tac shook his head, trying to clear his ears of the sound.

"It's a high A."

"So what?"

"That's hard to do."

"Let me try." Tac took the trumpet and puffed out his cheeks ready to blow.

"You're doing it wrong. Keep your lips small and don't puff out." Tac put his right hand around the valves and, red faced, blew hard, making his fingers go up and down on the valves. A whimper came out. "Give it back to me."

Tac held it away. "I want to try again." This time a real note came out. "See, I can do it." And he handed me the trumpet, satisfied with himself. "What note was that?"

"I don't know."

"Why not?"

"Don't talk. Then I'll finish sooner." I opened my book and propped it up against the table lamp.

Tac started spinning his army hat on his finger. "Maybe I'll play the saxophone. It's not so screechy."

"Trumpet isn't screechy."

"Oh, yeh? What about that A you played?"

"I was just showing you how high I could go."

"It was screechy."

"Why don't you go? You're bothering me."

"Saxophones are better."

"Shut up, Tac!"

"I'm going." And he put on his hat and went out the sliding door, not looking back.

"I'll be done in twenty minutes," I called after him.

"So what!"

That's the way it was. One minute we got along, the next thing you knew we were fighting. Then we were sorry. Maybe like brothers, I guessed.

After we got back from the beach, I went over to Tac's. He was out in back near the garden. He held a rifle and I thought maybe I should leave, but he saw me. "I'm not letting you touch this," he said, holding the rifle barrel down.

"I don't want to." I could just picture my mother seeing me with a gun. "Is it loaded?"

"Yeh, with points."

"What are they?"

"Little pellets with needles sticking up from them. Can put a hole in your hand or kill a rat stone dead."

"Can you do that?"

"Sure I can. We've got critters eating up the garden. I can shoot them as long as nobody's back here and my dad's home. But see, you came and spoiled it."

"I'll go." I looked at the rifle, wanting an excuse, anyway.

"You afraid?"

"Yeh."

"Good. You should be. You don't touch guns unless you know what to do." Tac started toward the house. "I'll unload this and put it away. We've got to see the man who runs the carnival."

"Why?"

"It opens tonight."

"So?"

"So he wants to talk to you."

"To me? What did you say to him?"

"I told him how you hit a high A."

"That's nothing."

"This morning you thought it was a big deal."

I looked at the rifle and didn't want to argue. "Put it away, okay?"

"Don't get all worked up. Go get your trumpet." Tac disappeared into the house while I worried about what he meant.

As we went down the street, Tac wouldn't tell me any more. We passed the cemetery and turned onto Main. Beach traffic was jammed up because the drawbridge to the mainland was open. Two more days and we'd have to leave, too.

Tac called out to people working at the docks and they waved back. I felt like an islander.

"We're going in two days," I said.

"When are you coming back?"

"Next summer."

"That stinks."

"I know. Maybe you can come up and visit me." I had been thinking that for a couple of days now.

"When?"

"I don't know. Just tell me why I have to take my trumpet to the carnival. I'm not playing."

"We'll get free rides."

"For doing what?"

"You'll see."

When we got there, the workers were setting up booths. The Ferris wheel was up and something with buckets and umbrellas was being put together. A tall thin man with a cowboy hat and boots was supervising.

"That's the man in charge of the whole thing," Tac said, pulling me along till we were standing next to him. "This is Steve," Tac said.

The man held out his hand. "Pleased to meet you," he said in Virginia talk. "You play the trumpet, Tac says."

"I'm learning."

Tac poked me in the arm. "Play something."

"Not here."

"Go ahead," the man said. "Make everyone stop working and listen."

There must have been at least thirty people there. "I'm not very good."

The man looked at his watch. "Boys, I have to get back to work."

Tac grabbed my case, opened it up, and handed me the trumpet and mouthpiece. "Play!" he said loudly.

That did it. Everyone was noticing us, anyway. I put the mouthpiece in and started playing "Yankee Doodle." It wasn't the Fourth of July but it was still July. I got as far as "stuck a feather in . . ." and the man held his hand up to stop me.

"Now announce something with notes."

"Announce something?"

"Like an important event. Do you know what I mean?"

This time I didn't press any valves. "Like that?"

"Perfect. How would you like free rides tonight?"

We worked from six to eight selling chances for a color TV. Tac shouted into a megaphone and I played flourishes on the trumpet. After the first few times, I wasn't embarrassed. Besides, nobody knew me there. We turned in the money whenever we got to fifty dollars. At eight we could go on the rides.

"Maybe we can do it again tomorrow night," Tac said as we walked to the head booth to drop off the last fifty dollars.

"I don't want to." I blew the spit out and worked the valves without making a sound. "That's my last night on the island."

"Then we'll stay till closing tonight."

"Can't. I have to be back by ten."

"That's not fair."

We gave the money to the man in charge and he gave us each a pass good on all the rides. We went on everything once and we were done by 8:50. It was

almost dark. The bay water across the street was still and black. The large fishing boats rested quietly, waiting for an early-morning trip, while the carnival kept going loud and fast.

"I'm getting my trumpet."

"You don't have to be home till ten."

"I want to go across to the bay."

"The carnival's only here till Saturday."

"That's how long I'll be here, too. Carnivals can be anywhere. Bays can't."

After I got the trumpet, we crossed the street and walked back toward the summer house. "I know a good place," Tac said, "where you can see the bay and nobody can see you." We went along Main till we were past the stores. "Right here." Tac turned into an alley between two old wooden warehouses. It led toward the bay and was narrow and dark.

I felt the oyster shells pushing into my sneakers. "I don't like it here."

"Yes, you do. Look there."

A single bulb hanging next to the door of one of the warehouses dimly lit the dock area. Tac walked to the edge and sat down, dangling his legs. I sat next to him.

The water lapped at the pier, and if there were any crabs, they kept to themselves. The lights across the bay were like sparklers, but the darkness over the water all but hid the few birds circling overhead. It was quiet. Tac looked at me. "Can you play taps?"

"I don't know." I took out my trumpet and put it to my lips. The music came in gentle waves, just right. It was okay to play and not get paid.

$\overline{7}$
The Storm

THAT night rain pounded against the windows and I pulled the spread up to my chin even though I wasn't cold. Lightning lit the room. I tried to remember. The dresser was near the hall door, the chair near the front window, the lamp was almost at the edge of the night table. I pulled it toward the center. Storms at home didn't bother me, but here they were too close with nothing familiar to take my mind off of them.

I pressed the light button on my watch. It was 3:25. I wondered what the beach was like now. Where did the birds go? Probably into the marshes to hide in the grasses. "Cord grass," Tac would say. "So, it's grass," I'd answer, "beach grass, marsh grass, lawn grass." Tac rode a power mower to cut his lawn. We still used a hand one, not even powered, at home. He'd laugh if he saw me pushing it. We were the only ones on the street who used one.

Lightning flashed, and this time the thunder followed before I could count. It was close. I pulled back the blinds and looked out. The pines on the edge of the property were waving wildly, their fuzzy tops looking like dust mops being shaken out. Then a gust drove a sheet of water against the window, sending me back under the covers. The hall door opened and my father walked in quietly.

"I'm awake," I whispered.

"I'm just checking the windows. You're not scared, are you?" He went from one window to the other.

"I can't sleep."

"It shouldn't last too long. I wonder what the beach is like."

"I was thinking that, too. We can go tomorrow, can't we?"

"You mean today. It'll be dawn pretty soon."

"We'll go, won't we? It's our last day."

"Sure. Now try to go to sleep." And he bent down to kiss me before leaving the room.

"I'm going to miss Tac," I said.

"You've gotten to be good friends."

"Do you think maybe he could come home with us?"

"Maybe. We'll talk about it during the day," my father whispered as he went out.

The day was sunny, as if nothing wild had happened during the night. There were some puddles next to the driveway. That's all. I went over to Tac's before breakfast. I didn't say anything about his maybe coming home with us, but I asked if he could go to the beach. He could, and we walked back to my house.

"I want to make eggs for you," he said. "I put cheese in them. Then I sprinkle in some garlic salt."

"That's gross."

If my mother didn't like the idea, she didn't say. She handed Tac the carton of eggs. "I don't have any garlic salt here and only a little cheese. I'm trying to finish up the food today so we won't have to take much home tomorrow."

"When are you leaving?"

"We have to be out of here by eleven."

"You can come to our house for breakfast tomorrow."

Tac cracked the eggs into a bowl.

"Did your mother tell you we talked a while last night?" My mother put a frying pan on the stove with a chunk of margarine in it.

"No, ma'am."

"She invited us to come for a cookout tonight."

"That's good." Tac poured the eggs into the pan. "Now don't talk. I have to concentrate." The eggs were okay, but Tac didn't have any. He said they were just for us.

The beach road was dry, but the water in the inlets was higher than usual. The road to the far end of the beach was blocked by sand washed down from the dunes, and we were directed to the closest parking lot.

Tac twirled his army hat on his finger. "There's going to be a surprise."

"What?"

"Wait'll you see the beach."

My father pulled into a space. "The waves will be rough."

"That's not all." Tac smiled a secretive smile. People were standing at the top of the ramps and stairs going over the dunes. "You know why nobody's going down?" We got out and I started to pull the beach spread with me. "You won't need it," Tac said, shoving it back onto the seat.

My father looked impatient. "Lock up and we'll go see what's what."

Tac and I ran ahead. At the top of the ramp, I looked in amazement. "Wow!"

The beach was a river with quiet pools oozing out on each side. Near the dunes there was only a narrow strip of sand to walk on, and that was wet. Water lapped high up around the signs and garbage cans, making it look as if they were in the wrong place instead of the water being out of bounds. On the other side of the river, toward the ocean, glassy wet sand stretched flat for about twenty feet till it broke off in a low ledge. Wild waves hitting the ledge sent foam and chunks of black junk into the air.

"There's no beach," I shouted back to my parents.

"Yeh, there is," Tac said. "It's just not a vacation beach. See how mad the water gets, tossing all those peat rollers back on shore?"

"What are peat rollers?"

"Old clumped-together marsh grass ripped up from down deep."

My parents came up next to us. I thought my mother would cry. "Tac, the beach is ruined."

"No, it's not. It'll dry."

"Not before we go."

"Maybe, maybe not." He went down the steps and stood on the steep slant of the dune. "It's fun this way."

My father walked to the edge of the water flowing in the channel. "Look at the fish."

Tac squatted down. "Anchovies!"

Better here than in salad, I thought.
The birds were already circling and div-
ing for the tiny treats.

People were moving past us now, wading across the river to the sand on the
other side. "Let's cross, too," I said. Tac
and I stepped into the gentle current. It
was up to our knees.

"Don't go near the waves," my mother
warned. "And stay in this area. No long
walks today."

The wet sand on the other side was like a mirror. We stamped and danced on it, staying away from the ledge that separated us from where the waves were furiously breaking.

The mist sprayed our faces and Tac tilted his hat forward. "Can't you stay longer?"

"We just rented the place for the week." I bent down and scooped up a handful of sand. A tiny crab crawled out of it and over my hand, trying to figure out what to do.

Tac let it walk onto his arm. "Silly mole crab. Look at its bug eyes." He bent down and brushed it onto the sand, and we watched it head fearlessly toward the water. "It doesn't know any better."

"Maybe you can come home with me."

"You mean tomorrow?"

"Do you want to?"

"Yeh, but how will I get back here?"

"I don't know. Maybe you can take a bus."

"I never took a bus alone."

"Are you scared to?"

"Of course not."

I turned around and saw my parents wading in one of the pools on the other side of the channel. "I asked my dad in the middle of the night and he said we'd talk about it today."

"I'd make eggs in the morning."

"Not with garlic."

"You're no fun."

"You can ride my sisters' bikes."

"I'm not riding any girl's bike."

"They're boys' bikes, ten speed."

"I don't need speeds."

"On hills you do."

"I forgot. Could we go see the Liberty Bell?"

"Maybe."

"Where would I sleep?"

"In my room. We have extra mattresses. You have to ask your parents, too."

Tac picked up a stick and started printing his name in the sand. "I was never away by myself, except to Gram's."

Tac stuck the stick straight into the sand. The shadow was short. The sky was full of sun and it was almost noon, the last noon we'd be here.

8
Going Home

IF I'd had to wear shoes, it would have ruined the vacation worse than practicing trumpet. Besides, I had just gotten new sneakers. Tac's mother had plates out on the back picnic table and his dad had the grill heating when we got there. Hamburgers and hot dogs were piled high next to a bowlful of squiggly, slimy-looking stuff. I looked at Tac. Then I tilted the bowl a little. "What is it?"

Tac's father smiled. "Oysters."

"What do you do with them?"

"Eat 'em. Haven't you had oysters this week?"

"No, sir," I said, sounding like Tac. I looked at the hamburgers sitting there looking normal, and I hoped I could just have one of them.

My mother came over and looked at the

oysters, too. "I've never cooked them," she said to Tac's father. "How do you do it?"

"I melt a little butter, toss them with bread crumbs and just brown them up. Nothing's better than fresh fried oysters."

"I can't wait to try them," my mother said. I thought that was going a little too far.

Just then Tac's mother pushed open the kitchen door with a full tray. My mother went up to her to help and Tac tugged at my sleeve. "I want to ask you something."

We went around front. Tac was anxious. "Did you talk about my going home with you?"

"Sort of."

"What do you mean, sort of? What'd they say?"

"It was fine with them as long as your parents would let you, but we'd have to figure out how to get you home."

"Yowee!" Tac galloped around the lawn and then came back. "It's okay with mine, but they said not to say anything till they talked to your parents tonight."

When we went around back again, the

hamburgers were on one side of the grill and a heavy skillet with oysters was on the other side. I hoped the smells would stay separate.

"There you are," Tac's mother said. "We were wondering where you two went. Well, Tac, how do you feel about taking a bus home from Steve's?"

"You mean I can go?"

"If you don't mind traveling home on your own. It's five hours."

"We'd pack some food for you," my mother assured him.

"Yeh." I added. "Eggs with garlic salt."

He ignored me. "Where would I get the bus?"

"About sixty miles from our house," my father said. "That way you won't have to transfer. We'll drive you there and see to it you're on the right bus that comes straight down Route 13 to Perkins Corner."

"There'll be stops along the way," Tac's mother added, "so you have to read signs to make sure you don't get off too soon or go too far and end up at Virginia Beach."

"How long will I stay?"

"About a week," Tac's father said. "How does that sound to you?"

Tac looked at me. "How does that sound to you?"

"That's good." I turned to my parents. "Do you think we could go to Philadelphia one day?"

Tac's mother interrupted. "Everything's ready to eat. We can talk after we have our plates full."

I tried an oyster, and even swallowed it to be polite, but I concentrated on a hamburger and a hot dog after that.

When we left, we drove out to the beach for the last time to see the sunset over the water. Then we went back to the house that would be someone else's next week.

In the morning I woke up to a knock on the sliding glass door. It was too early, I was sure, and I turned away from it. "You in there?" the familiar voice called.

I struggled to open my eyes. There was another knock. "Hey, Steve, you in there?"

I looked at my watch. It was 7:05. "I'm coming."

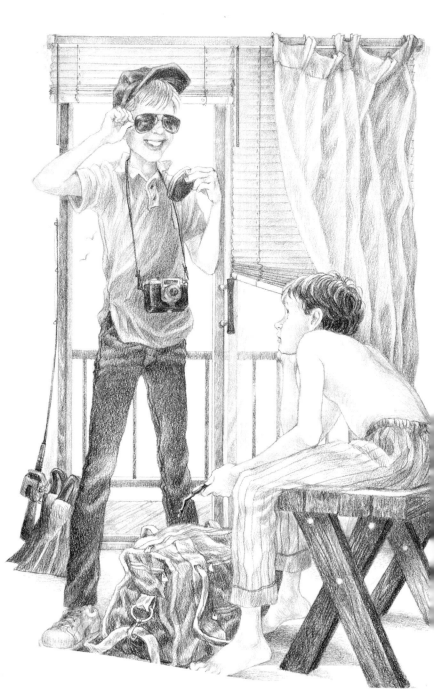

I got up and unlocked the door. ''It's too early, Tac.''

''No, it's not. We have to get going.'' He lifted up a large bag with lots of zipper sections on the outside and dropped it in front of me. ''I brought jeans and shorts, mostly, and my camera. My mom made me take good shoes, but I'm not wearing them. Got my hat, too.'' And he patted it gently on his head. ''Look at this.'' He took a zipper case out of his pocket. ''Folding shades.'' He unfolded them and put them on.

I rubbed my eyes. ''When did you get up?''

''About six. How come you're not ready?''

There was no use answering.

We were packed to go by eleven. My father checked the bikes on the roof rack and everything was tight. Tac and I sat in the back with food his mother had given us for the trip, at least a week's supply of cheese, a bag of cookies, and bananas. We drove slowly down the oyster-shell driveway for the last time and, waving a last good-bye to Tac's parents, headed for the bridge to the mainland. I looked at the fishing boats bouncing in the bay and wondered what Tac would think of a place without ocean.

"How long did you say it would take?" he asked.

"Five and a half hours with a stop," my father answered.

"That's too long."

My mother was concerned. "Do you want us to turn around and take you back, Tac?"

"No way." Then he looked at me. "How high are the hills near your house?"

"Higher than that mast." I pointed to the clam boat next to the bridge.

"Mast! You know big words."

"Stop it. How about ice skating when we get home?"

"In the summer?"

"There's an indoor rink in town."

"I never ice-skated."

"I'll teach you." And we drove on the low road through the marsh away from the island. Vacation wasn't over. There was still another week to go.